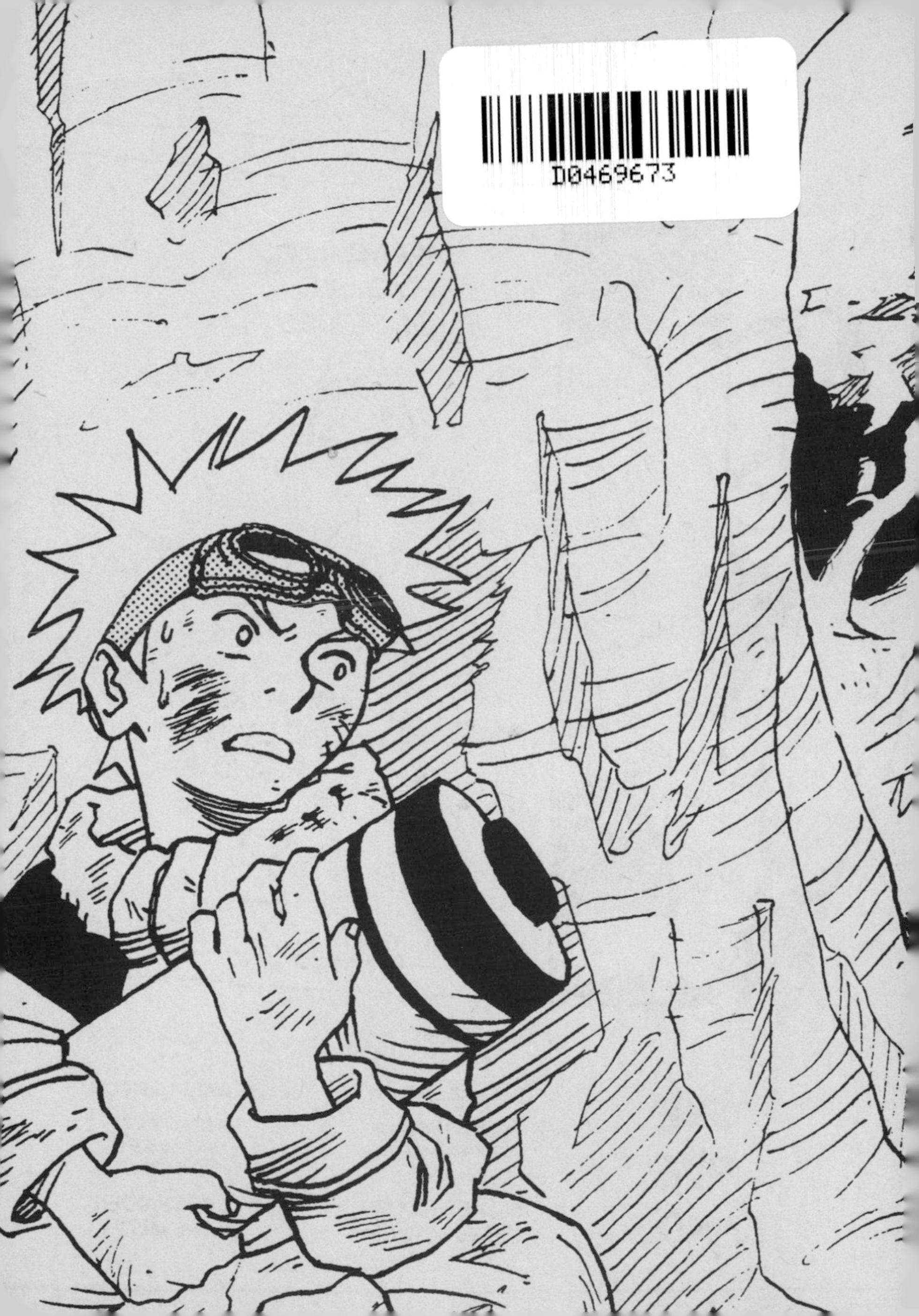

IWA NO KUNI:
THE LAND
OF STONES

SUNA NO KUNI:
THE LAND
OF SAND

THE
FIVE
LANDS

THE FIRE SHADOW

KONOHA NO KUNI
KONOHAGAKURE
NO SATO:

VILLAGE HIDDEN
IN THE LEAVES

THE WATER SHADOW

KIRO NO KUNI
KIRIGAKURE
NO SATO:

VILLAGE HIDDEN
IN THE MIST

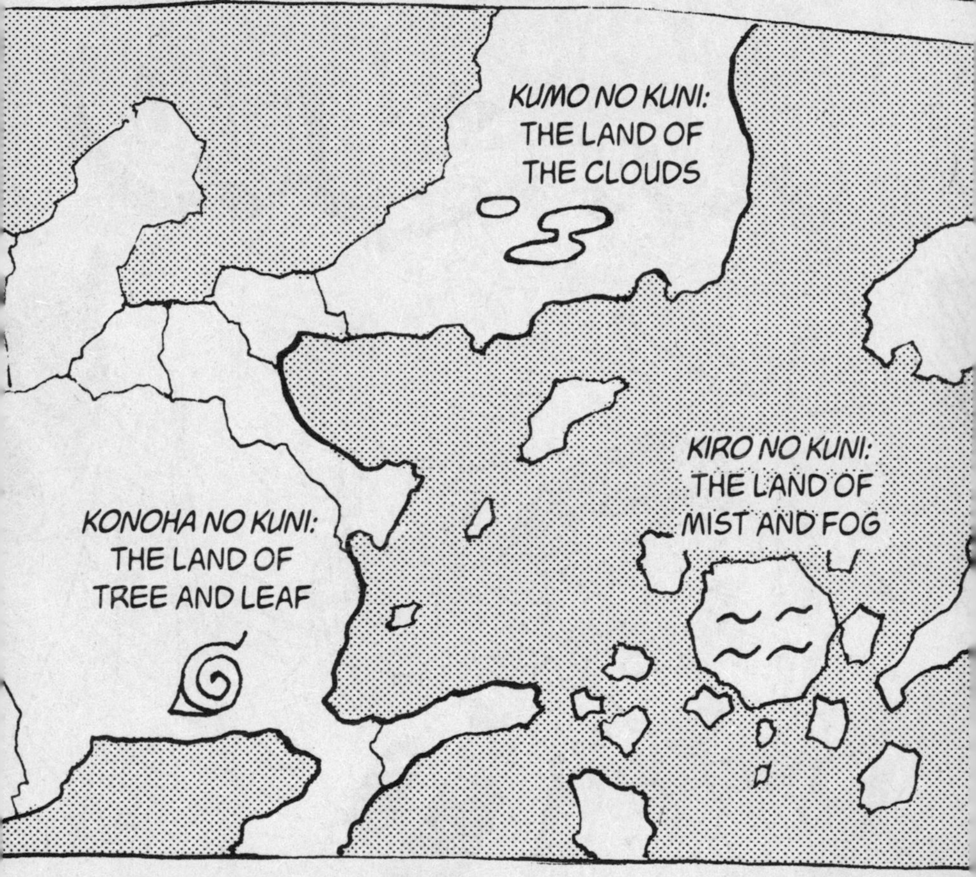

KUMO NO KUNI:
THE LAND OF
THE CLOUDS
KIRO NO KUNI:
THE LAND OF
MIST AND FOG
KONOHA NO KUNI:
THE LAND OF
TREE AND LEAF

THE LIGHTNING SHADOW

KUMO NO KUNI
KUMOGAKURE
NO SATO:

VILLAGE HIDDEN
IN THE CLOUDS

THE WIND SHADOW

SUNA NO KUNI
SUNAGAKURE
NO SATO:

VILLAGE HIDDEN
IN THE SAND

THE EARTH SHADOW

IWA NO KUNI
IWAGAKURE
NO SATO:

VILLAGE HIDDEN
IN THE SHADOW

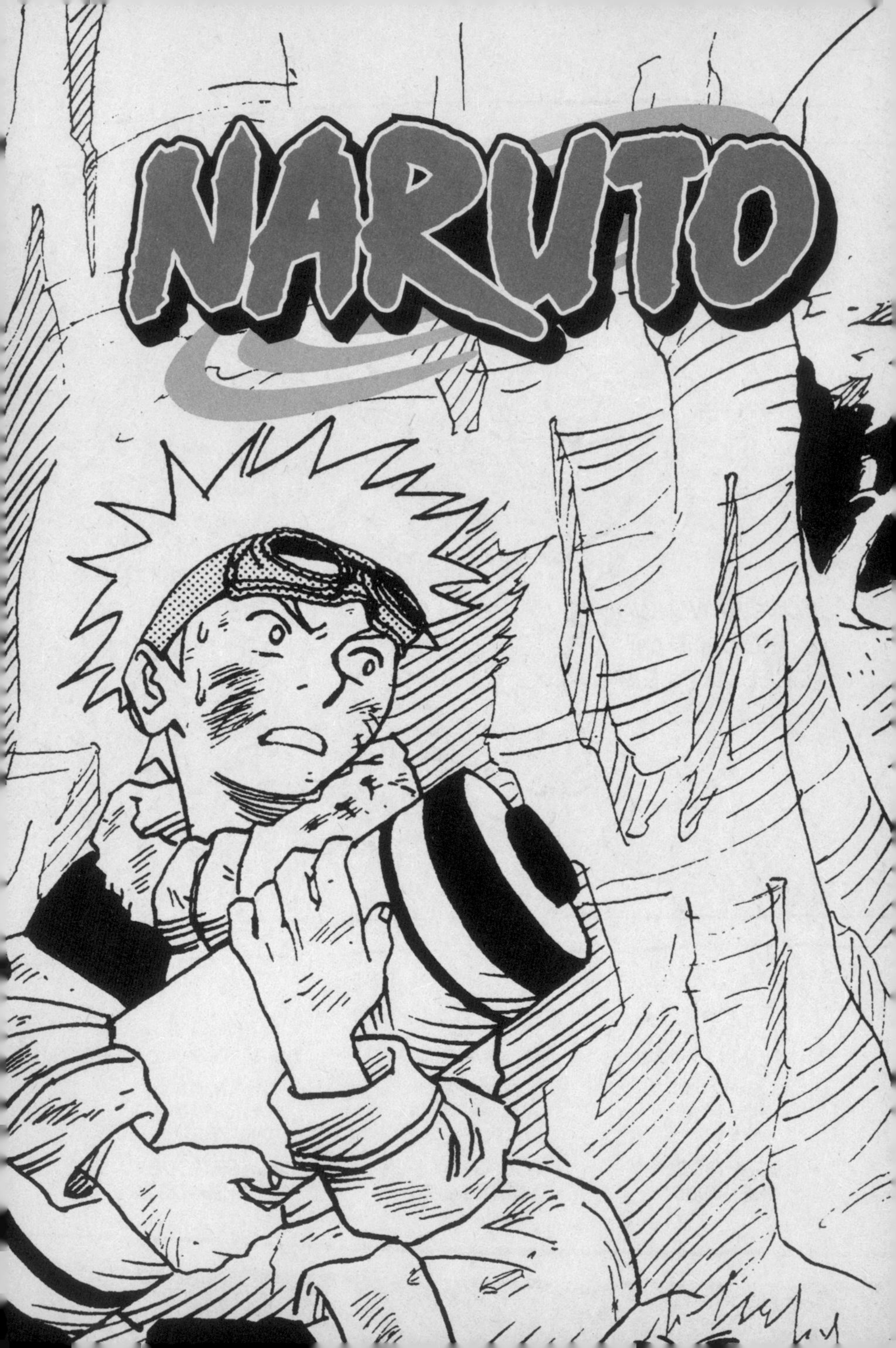
NARUTO

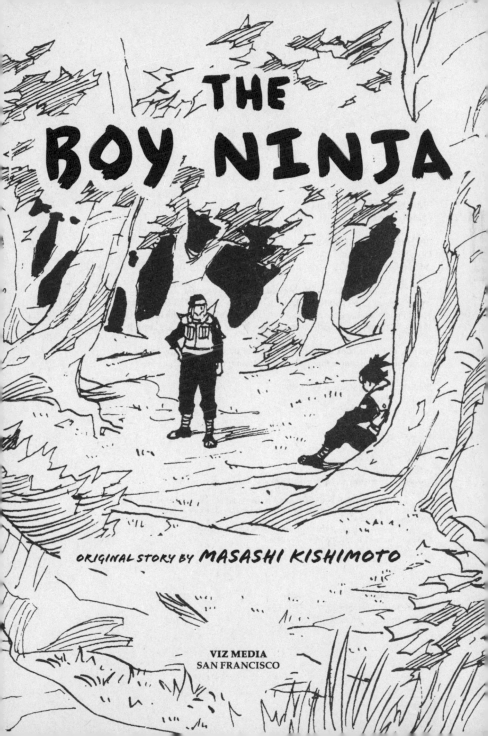

THE BOY NINJA

ORIGINAL STORY BY **MASASHI KISHIMOTO**

VIZ MEDIA
SAN FRANCISCO

NARUTO THE BOY NINJA
CHAPTER BOOK 1

Illustrations: Masashi Kishimoto
Design: Courtney Utt
Adaptation: Tracey West

NARUTO © 1999 by Masashi Kishimoto. All rights reserved.
Original manga first published in Japan in 1999 by SHUEISHA Inc., Tokyo.
This English language chapter book novelization is based on the original manga. The
stories, characters and incidents mentioned in this publication are entirely fictional.

Published by VIZ Media, LLC
P.O. Box 77010
San Francisco, CA 94107

www.viz.com

West, Tracey, 1965-
 The boy ninja / original story by Masashi Kishimoto ; adapted by Tracey West.
     p. cm.
 Summary: While training to be a ninja, jokester Naruto fails his final exam, but when a crisis
occurs in the ninja village, he realizes that he has what it takes to become a ninja.
 ISBN 978-1-4215-2056-8
[1. Ninja--Fiction. 2. Self-perception--Fiction. 3. Courage--Fiction.] I.
Kishimoto, Masashi. II. Title. PZ7.W51937Bo 2008
[Fic]--dc22
              2007050281

Printed in the U.S.A.
First printing, October 2008
Third printing, October 2019

THE LEAF VILLAGE sat deep inside a green valley, surrounded by mountains. It was a perfect setting for the ninja who trained there. They kept the village safe and protected. It was usually a quiet and peaceful place.

Usually...

"Ha ha ha!" A taunting laugh rang through the valley. The villagers looked up to see a boy high atop one of the mountain faces. His bright yellow hair stuck out in spikes on the top of his head. A pair of thick goggles was

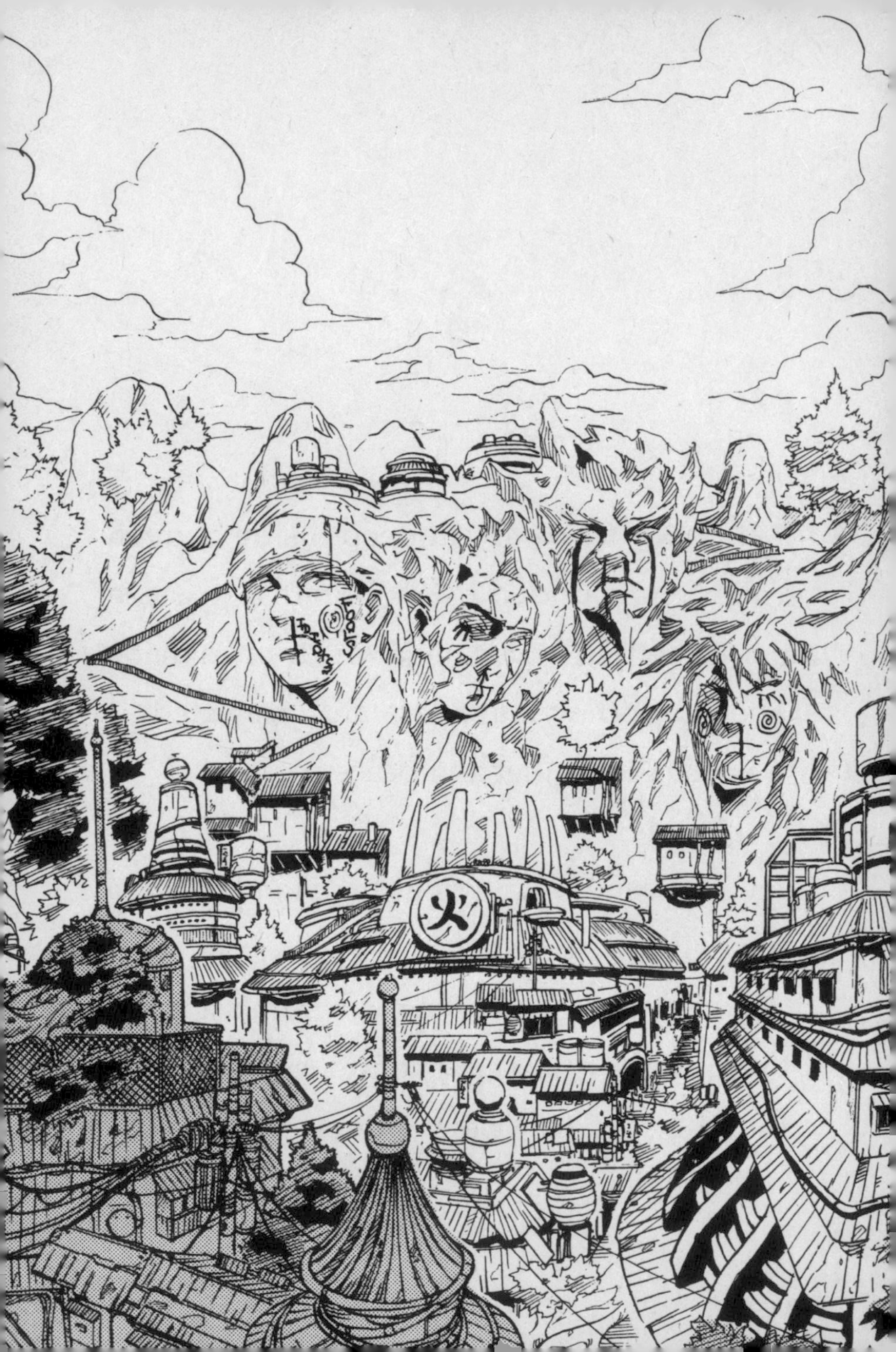

strapped around his forehead. A rope was tied around his waist. And his blue eyes were bright with mischief. He had a grin on his face as he dangled in front of the giant stone heads carved into the rock.

The boy had a bucket of paint and a paintbrush. He swung back and forth across the faces, laughing. He painted a beard on one face, then a black eye on another. One fierce-looking hero had a line of paint running from his nose.

One of the villagers pointed at the boy. "IT'S NARUTO!"

Two men ran to the home of Lord Hokage, the leader of the village. Only the wisest and bravest ninja of all could become the Hokage. The one who earned the title was charged with leading the village.

The current leader of the Leaf Village was also known as the Third Hokage because there had been two Hokage before him. Age had whitened his hair and carved lines into his thin face. When the two men arrived, he was painting a scroll.

"LORD HOKAGE!" the men cried.

"What is it?" the Hokage replied. But he knew the answer already. "Some new prank by Naruto, I presume?" "He's putting graffiti on the mountain faces!" one of the men reported.

"In paint!" the second man yelled.

Lord Hokage sighed. It was always something with Naruto Uzumaki. That boy had been nothing but trouble since the day he was born.

A small crowd had gathered below Naruto by this time.

"Enough with the stupid pranks!" someone shouted up at him.

"You are so dead when they catch you! You know that?" another person called out.

The words just bounced off Naruto.

"Losers! Wannabes!" he yelled back. "You don't have what it takes to do something this low. I rule, and you drool!"

The crowd parted as Lord Hokage came through. "How dare you!" he scolded Naruto. "Who do you think you are?"

A tall ninja ran up behind the Hokage. A headband with a leaf symbol was wrapped around his forehead. His black hair was

pulled into a small ponytail at the back of his
head.

"Lord Hokage, I can't apologize enough,"
the ninja said. He looked up at Naruto. The
boy was painting a bull's-eye on the cheek of
one of the stone faces.

"What do you think you're doing, you
idiot?" he yelled. "Get down from there and
get back to class!"

The familiar voice struck Naruto like an arrow.

It's my teacher, Master Iruka, Naruto realized. I'M IN BIG TROUBLE!

NARUTO SAT ON the floor in the front of his classroom. His arms were tied behind his back. Master Iruka wasn't taking any chances. He towered over Naruto, his arms folded across his chest.

"Tomorrow, all of your classmates will graduate from the Ninja Academy. But you have failed every course you took in the secret arts." Iruka's voice grew louder. "So you chose today for your stupid tricks?!"

"Sir, yes, sir!" Naruto answered, in a

mocking tone. He refused to look at Iruka.

Why should he bother to study? He didn't have a mom or dad. Everyone in the village

hated him. It didn't matter what he did—so he might as well have some fun.

Master Iruka cares, whispered a small voice deep inside him. But Naruto pushed away the thought. Iruka was a sensei, or teacher. It was his job to boss around his students.

Master Iruka glared down at Naruto. The boy's brain was as thick as stone. There was no point in yelling at him. If he failed, he failed.

The teacher turned his attention to the class. "Today, we review the art of transformation."

"WHAT?" the students shouted. Transforming was one of the most difficult secret arts. They'd already practiced it. But now they would have to do it again. Everyone shot dirty looks at Naruto.

"All you have to do is make yourself look just like me," Master Iruka told them.

He untied Naruto as the students lined up. The first student stepped forward. A look of concentration crossed the boy's face. He spun around quickly, crying out.

A funnel of wind whipped up around him. There was a loud **BONG**, like the sound of a deep bell. The wind died down. And where the boy once stood was a second Master Iruka. He had the same face, the same hair, and the same headband. He even wore dark blue pants and a shirt under a thick vest, just like the teacher.

"Well done!" Master Iruka said. "Next up, Uzumaki Naruto."

Naruto stepped up. Behind him, his classmates frowned.

"This is all your fault," one of them hissed.

"This stinks," Naruto muttered. "But here goes nothing."

There was a gleam in his eye as he steadied himself for the transformation. He planted his feet on the floor, legs apart. Then he cried out.

"CHANGE!"

Wind swirled around the room. A loud **BONG** filled the classroom. Then the wind died down. Naruto had transformed…

…into a cute girl with blonde ponytails!

The girl giggled and blew a kiss to Master Iruka.

The teacher's face turned as white as snow. He nearly fainted from the shock.

Naruto quickly transformed back and laughed.

Master Iruka's face turned from white to bright red. He was angry now.

"How big a fool are you?" he screamed. "A jutsu is a secret ninja technique—a skill to help you in battle. But you waste all of your time and talent inventing these stupid tricks!"

He grabbed Naruto by the arm.

"You come with me," he growled.

ONCE AGAIN, NARUTO dangled in front of the faces carved into the mountain. This time, he wasn't painting them. He was scrubbing off the paint. He stood on a platform that hung from ropes from the top of the mountain. He stuck a brush into a bucket of soapy water, pulled it out, and scrubbed the graffiti.

"Rats," Naruto muttered. "Double rats!"

Iruka sat on top of the mountain. He watched Naruto work.

"You will not leave here until every drop

of paint is gone!" Iruka shouted.

"So? It's not like there's anyone at home waiting for me!" Naruto shouted back.

Iruka suddenly felt less angry. He knew Naruto had a tough life. And he was just a boy, after all. He rubbed the scar that ran across the top of his nose, thinking.

"Naruto," Iruka said.

Naruto looked up. "Now what?"

"When you're done, I'll buy you a bowl of ramen noodles," the sensei told him.

Naruto's mood changed. "All right!" he cheered. Ramen was his favorite food. His mouth watered as he thought about the delicious, hot noodle soup. "Ramen, here I come!"

Naruto scrubbed as quickly as he could.

Still, it took hours to wash off all the paint. It was dark by the time Iruka took him to the ramen restaurant.

The busy restaurant was just a small hut in the center of the village. Inside, a cook made the ramen. Outside, customers sat on stools. They ate their meals at a long counter.

Naruto ordered the biggest bowl of soup on the menu. He picked up the noodles with his chopsticks. Then he loudly slurped them down. When he finished the noodles, he picked up the bowl and gulped down the hot, steaming broth.

Iruka shook his head. He had never seen a human eat like that before. He also noticed that Naruto was not wearing his goggles. That was strange too. Naruto always wore his goggles.

"Naruto," he said. "Why did you paint graffiti on the mountain faces? Don't you know who the Hokage are?"

"Of course," Naruto replied. "They were the best ninja in the village!"

Naruto thought back to the faces carved

into the mountain. His favorite one was a man with a serious face and spiky hair. "The Fourth Lord Hokage saved our town," Naruto went on. "He beat the Nine-Tailed Fox Spirit."

"So if you know how important they are, why did you do it?" Iruka asked.

"Because someday, they'll call *me* Lord Hokage!" Naruto cried. He pointed his chopsticks at Iruka. **"I AM GOING TO BE THE BEST HOKAGE EVER!** Then everyone in town will have to respect me."

Naruto slurped down the last bit of soup. Then he faced Iruka. He put his palms together in front of him to show respect.

"By the way, Sensei, I need a favor," Naruto said.

"Another bowl of ramen?" Iruka guessed.

"No. I want your leaf headband," Naruto said. "Pretty please?"

Iruka touched the dark blue headband he wore around his head. The leaf symbol was carved into a piece of silver metal. The metal was attached to the fabric.

"My leaf headband? No way," Iruka said. "I can't just give one to you. You have to graduate from Ninja Academy to get a leaf headband. You need to pass your test tomorrow."

Naruto frowned. He knew he wasn't going to pass his test. He would never get a leaf headband!

"Is that why you took off your goggles?" Iruka asked with a grin. It was true. Naruto had been so sure he'd get his headband that

he had already taken off his goggles in antici-
pation of wearing the band.

Naruto scowled. "Another bowl of ramen
here!" he yelled.

NARUTO SLUMPED DOWN in his chair. He put his head on his desk and sighed.

The other students in class looked happy. Today was their final test. Soon they would be real ninja!

Master Iruka came into the room. "For your final test, you must each make a doppelganger, an exact copy of yourself," he announced. "Wait here until we call your name. Then come into the next room."

Naruto groaned. Why did it have to be

doppelgangers? He was terrible at making copies of himself. There was no way he was going to pass.

The students were called in one by one. Each one came back holding a leaf headband. Jealousy swelled up inside Naruto. He wanted a headband so badly!

Then Naruto heard his name. He walked into the room next to the classroom. Master Iruka sat at a desk in the front of the room. Next to him sat Master Mizuki, another teacher. With his pale blond hair and blue eyes, Mizuki was Iruka's exact opposite.

The leaf headbands were laid out in rows on the desk. Naruto took a deep breath. He would get a headband. He was not going to fail!

"Here goes nothing," he said.

He planted his feet firmly on the floor. He closed his eyes and concentrated. Naruto had to make an exact copy of himself appear next to him. Other kids could make three copies. Naruto had never even made one. But he had to try. His future depended on it.

"*Grrrrrr...*" Naruto growled as beads of sweat ran down his face. He raised his arms above his head.

"Behold! A perfect doppelganger!"

A loud **BONG** filled the air. Something appeared next to Naruto. Naruto nervously turned his head to look. Had he done it?

The thing lying on the floor looked like Naruto...if Naruto were made out of cookie dough. The doppelganger had Naruto's blond hair and blue eyes. But its tongue hung out of its mouth. It flopped around on the floor like a fish.

Naruto's heart sank. A copy was supposed to look exactly like you, so you could fool enemies in battle. This lump of dough wouldn't fool anybody.

Master Iruka's face turned red. Why did Naruto get everything wrong?

"YOU FAIL!" Iruka yelled.

"Master Iruka," Mizuki said gently, "Naruto has taken this test three times. He did manage to create a double of himself, even if it wasn't that great. Maybe we could give him a break."

A burst of hope filled Naruto's heart. Would he get his leaf headband after all?

"The answer is no, Master Mizuki," Iruka said firmly. "Naruto was supposed to make three doppelgangers. He only made one, and he did it very badly. He does not deserve to pass."

Naruto stomped out of the room. Why did he think his teacher or sensei, Master Iruka, would give him a break? His sensei was always so hard on him.

It felt good to be angry with Master Iruka. It kept other thoughts out of his head. Thoughts like the fact that he didn't get a leaf headband. He would never become a ninja now. The people of the village would never respect him.

That afternoon, there was a celebration at Ninja Academy. All the students and their families were there.

Naruto sat on a swing hanging from a tree and watched from a distance. He didn't have anything better to do. The students' brand-new leaf headbands gleamed in the afternoon sun. Naruto could hear proud parents praise their children.

"Great job, son! Your old man is proud."

"Congratulations, graduate! Tonight we're going to celebrate!"

The words stung. Nobody was proud of Naruto. Nobody was going to do anything special for him. It had been that way as long as Naruto could remember. And it was never going to change.

New voices drifted through the air. Two women from the village were talking about Naruto in loud whispers.

"That's the kid who failed," the first woman said.

"Serves him right," said the second woman. "Can you imagine if they let someone like that become a ninja? I mean, think about what he is."

"Don't say that!" the first woman scolded. "We're not supposed to talk about it."

Naruto ran from the swing, tears stinging his eyes. He didn't want to hear any more.

He ran through the streets of the village. He wasn't sure where he was going. He just wanted to be far away from all his happy classmates and their proud parents. He put his goggles back on his head.

"Naruto!" Naruto heard Master Mizuki's voice behind him. He stopped and turned. Had his teacher followed him here?

"Come on," Mizuki said. "Let's find a place to talk."

They sat on the high balcony of a nearby building. They could see the whole village below them. Naruto felt calm for the first time all day.

"You need to understand Master Iruka," Mizuki said. "His parents died when he was very young. He has worked hard to become a teacher. He did it by himself. Nobody helped him."

"So what does that have to do with me?" Naruto asked.

"YOU REMIND HIM OF HIMSELF," Mizuki explained. "He thinks he is helping you to grow strong. Try to understand. Can't you give him a break, from one orphan to another?"

Naruto didn't feel like being understanding. "I just really wanted to graduate," he said sadly.

Mizuki eyed Naruto for a moment. "Then

I guess I have no choice."

"What do you mean?" Naruto asked.

Master Mizuki leaned closer to Naruto. "Let me tell you a secret…"

A BRIGHT MOON shone over the village. Naruto quietly walked down the street. Earlier today, he thought he had no future. He thought he had nobody to help him.

But Master Mizuki had changed all that. Soon, everything would be different.

Naruto stopped in front of Lord Hokage's house. The old man would be asleep by now. Naruto crept around the house until he saw an open window. Carefully, he climbed inside.

The room was dark. Naruto wasn't sure which room he was in. Master Mizuki had said to find the library. He tiptoed across the floor.

Suddenly, the room was bright with light from a lantern.

"What are you doing in my house in the middle of the night?" a voice asked.

Naruto spun around. Lord Hokage stood there, angry. Naruto panicked. He couldn't get caught. Not now. Not when he was so close.

Naruto closed his eyes and used the only jutsu he knew.

"Behold!" Naruto cried.

The sight of Naruto changing into a cute little girl caught Lord Hokage by surprise.

He fainted from the shock.

Naruto changed back into himself. He felt bad about scaring Lord Hokage like that—

but not *too* bad. Now he had time to find the library.

Naruto ran from room to room until he found what he was looking for. Shelves lined every wall of the library. Hundreds of scrolls were tucked into the shelves. Naruto scanned the piles of scrolls. Luckily, Master Mizuki had told him where to look.

"GOTCHA!" Naruto grabbed the scroll from the shelf. He ran to the nearest window and climbed out.

His heart was pounding. He had done it! All he had to do was get to the secret place Mizuki had told him about. He raced down the street.

Naruto was too excited to notice the mysterious figure watching him from the shadows of the street. The person smiled and nodded.

So far, the plan was working...

6

MASTER IRUKA LAY on his bed, wide awake in the middle of the night. Graduation day was usually a happy day. But seeing how sad Naruto had looked made him sad too. Usually Naruto acted like nothing bothered him. But today Naruto seemed to have given up. It was hard for Iruka to see him like that.

Lord Hokage had talked to Iruka after the graduation ceremony. The Hokage's words ran through his mind now.

"I understand how you feel about the boy," Lord Hokage had said. **"You two are alike.** Both of you grew up without parents."

Iruka thought back to when he was a child. He had never forgotten how the Fox Spirit attacked his village. Iruka still remembered the Fox Spirit's glowing eyes and sharp teeth. Its nine tails whipped around its body, hitting everything in their path.

His mother and father were both skilled ninja. They had both fought the demon bravely, trying to protect the village. Iruka ran to them, wanting to help. But one of the village men had grabbed him and pulled him away. He never saw his parents again.

Suddenly, there was a loud knock on the door. Iruka sat up. Who could be visiting at this time of the night? He opened the door to see Master Mizuki standing there.

"What are you doing here?" Iruka asked.

"It's Naruto," Mizuki said. His face was serious. "Somehow he found out about the Scroll of Sealing. He just stole it from Lord Hokage!"

Iruka turned pale. "It can't be!" Naruto played a lot of pranks. But he had never done anything this dangerous.

The two teachers ran to the house of Lord Hokage. He was waiting for them. His most trusted ninja surrounded him.

"Is it true?" Iruka asked.

Lord Hokage nodded. "Yes. Naruto has stolen the Scroll of Sealing."

The ninja were angry. "Lord Hokage,

Naruto has gone too far this time!" one of them yelled.

The village leader did not disagree. "The scroll he has taken is very dangerous," Lord Hokage said. "The very first Hokage of the village sealed it away years ago. In the wrong hands, it could be deadly."

Lord Hokage faced the ninja. "Go! WE MUST FIND HIM!"

The men charged down the village streets. Their anger worried Iruka. If they found Naruto, they might hurt him. Naruto had done something dumb, but he was only a boy. Iruka would have to find Naruto before anyone else did.

Where would Naruto go? He had no friends, no family. Iruka thought back to when

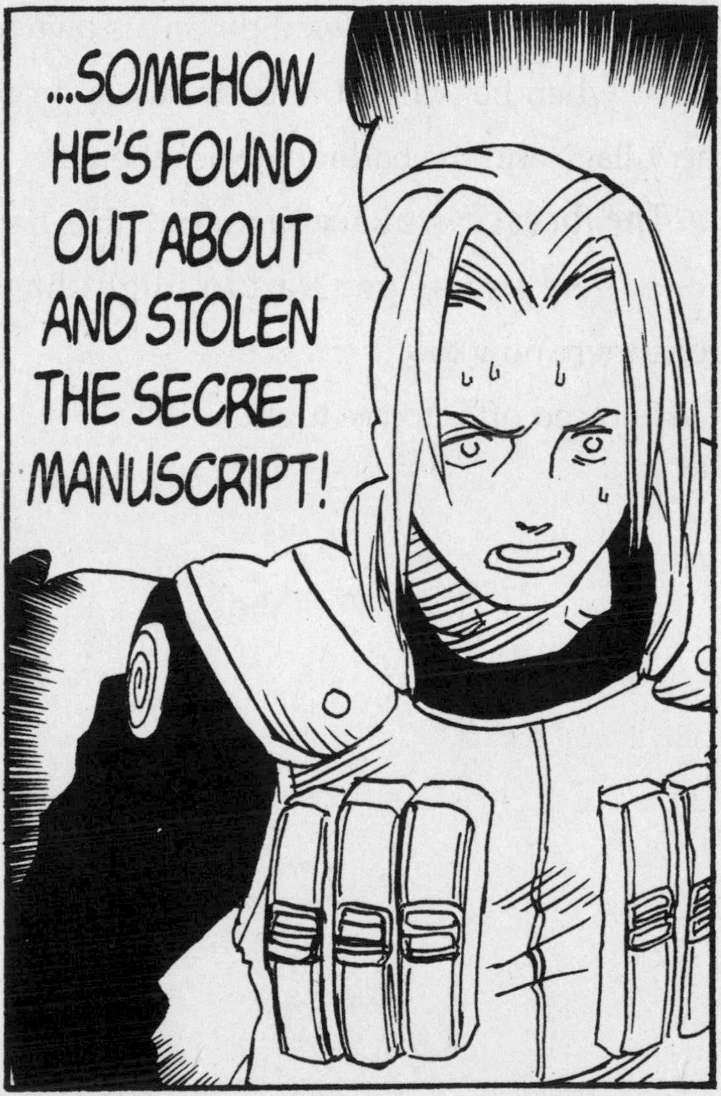
...SOMEHOW HE'S FOUND OUT ABOUT AND STOLEN THE SECRET MANUSCRIPT!

he was a boy. He often went off on his own to think, when he wanted to be far away from the village and the bad memories there.

"*The forest,*" Iruka whispered. He had gone there years ago. Naruto might have gone there now too.

He raced off into the night.

NARUTO SAT ON the forest ground, panting. He had been in the secret place all night long. The sun was just starting to rise. An eerie green light bathed the small clearing. Behind Naruto was the abandoned shack Mizuki had told him about.

Naruto was tired, but he felt good. The scroll held the instructions for amazing secret jutsu. Naruto practiced one of the jutsu for hours. He had never practiced so hard in his life. Now the scroll was rolled up and strapped to his back. He closed his eyes, trying to memorize what he had just learned.

"Gotcha!"

Iruka stood over Naruto. **"I found you!"** he cried.

"That's okay, because I was just about to find *you*," Naruto said. He jumped to his feet, smiling.

Iruka was confused. Naruto was a thief in hiding. Iruka had just caught him. Why wasn't he running away?

"Too bad you found me so fast," Naruto said. "I only had time to learn one technique."

Iruka was even more confused now. "What have you been doing? You look really tired."

"Wait, I'll show you," Naruto said. His blue eyes gleamed with excitement. "I never knew how amazing ninja moves could be!"

"You were practicing a jutsu?" Iruka asked. Naruto looked like he had been working all night.

Naruto didn't answer. His eyes were closed in concentration. He didn't want to stop practicing.

"Naruto, what is that scroll on your back?" Iruka asked.

Naruto opened his eyes. "Master Mizuki

told me about it," Naruto said. "He told me about this place too. He said if I could learn one of the jutsu in this scroll, you would let me graduate."

"Mizuki?" Iruka was stunned. So that's how Naruto had learned about the scroll. But why would Mizuki tell him? Unless...

A sudden storm of throwing knives, called kunai, flew through the air. Iruka quickly pushed Naruto out of the way. But he was too late to save himself.

The sharp knives pinned Iruka to the wall of the shack. Iruka cried out.

Iruka and Naruto looked to see where the kunai had come from. Mizuki stood on the branch of a nearby tree. There was a cruel look on his face.

"I didn't expect you to find this place, Iruka," he said.

"Now I understand!" Iruka cried.

Mizuki ignored Iruka. He fixed his eyes on Naruto. The boy stared up at his teacher, afraid and confused.

"Naruto, give me the scroll!" Mizuki demanded.

NARUTO WAS TOO dazed to respond. Iruka's eyes shone with fury. Sweat poured down his face.

"Don't let him have it, Naruto!" Iruka shouted. "Protect that scroll with your life. It's more dangerous than you know. That scroll has the secret of a forbidden ninja art."

Mizuki looked down on them from the tree branch. There was an angry scowl on his face. Taking the scroll from Naruto would have been so easy. But now he had to deal with Iruka too.

"Mizuki used you because he wanted it for himself!" Iruka cried.

Naruto jumped to his feet. His mind scrambled to make sense of what was happening. Master Mizuki had been so nice to him. He'd helped him. Master Iruka didn't even want him to graduate. Could Master Mizuki really have tricked him?

"Naruto, even if you read the scroll, it won't make sense to you," Mizuki said, his voice smooth. "Let me explain something to you."

Naruto didn't know what to think. Suddenly, the scroll felt like a heavy weight on his back.

"Shut up, you fool!" Iruka screamed up at

Mizuki. He struggled to free himself from the kunai. The wound in his leg kept him from fighting. All he had were his words—and the hope that Naruto would somehow hear the truth.

Mizuki ignored him. He kept his eyes fixed on Naruto. "You know what really happened when the Fox Spirit was sealed up twelve years ago, don't you?" he asked. "Since that day, the people in the village have been bound by a strict rule."

"I don't remember any rule," Naruto protested.

"You wouldn't," Mizuki said with a sinister smile. "Part of that rule was that everyone would know about it. Everyone—except you."

"Except me?" Naruto asked, his voice rising with anger. "Why not me? What rule are you talking about?"

Mizuki didn't answer. He looked down, and a low, mean laugh rose from his throat.

"What?" Naruto yelled. Panic gripped him. He had a feeling he didn't want to know the answer—but he had to know, just the same. "What was the rule? What? Tell me!"

Mizuki locked eyes with Naruto. "That no one must ever tell you what you really are— the Demon Fox!"

The words stung Naruto like a knife. "What are you talking about?"

"You are the Nine-Tailed Fox that destroyed the village!" Mizuki crowed.

A strange buzzing filled Naruto's ears. He felt like he was in some terrible dream.

"The Fourth Hokage trapped the demon inside you," Mizuki shouted over Iruka's protests. "Since then, you've been made a fool of by everyone in town!"

Naruto couldn't move or speak as Mizuki's words surrounded him. He wanted it to be a lie, but deep inside him, Naruto knew it was true. Somehow, he'd always known he was different.

"Didn't you think it was strange? Everyone seems to hate you, wherever you go," Mizuki continued. "If he were honest, even noble Iruka would admit he hates you too!"

He took a windmill shuriken, a giant throwing star, from his back. Naruto was

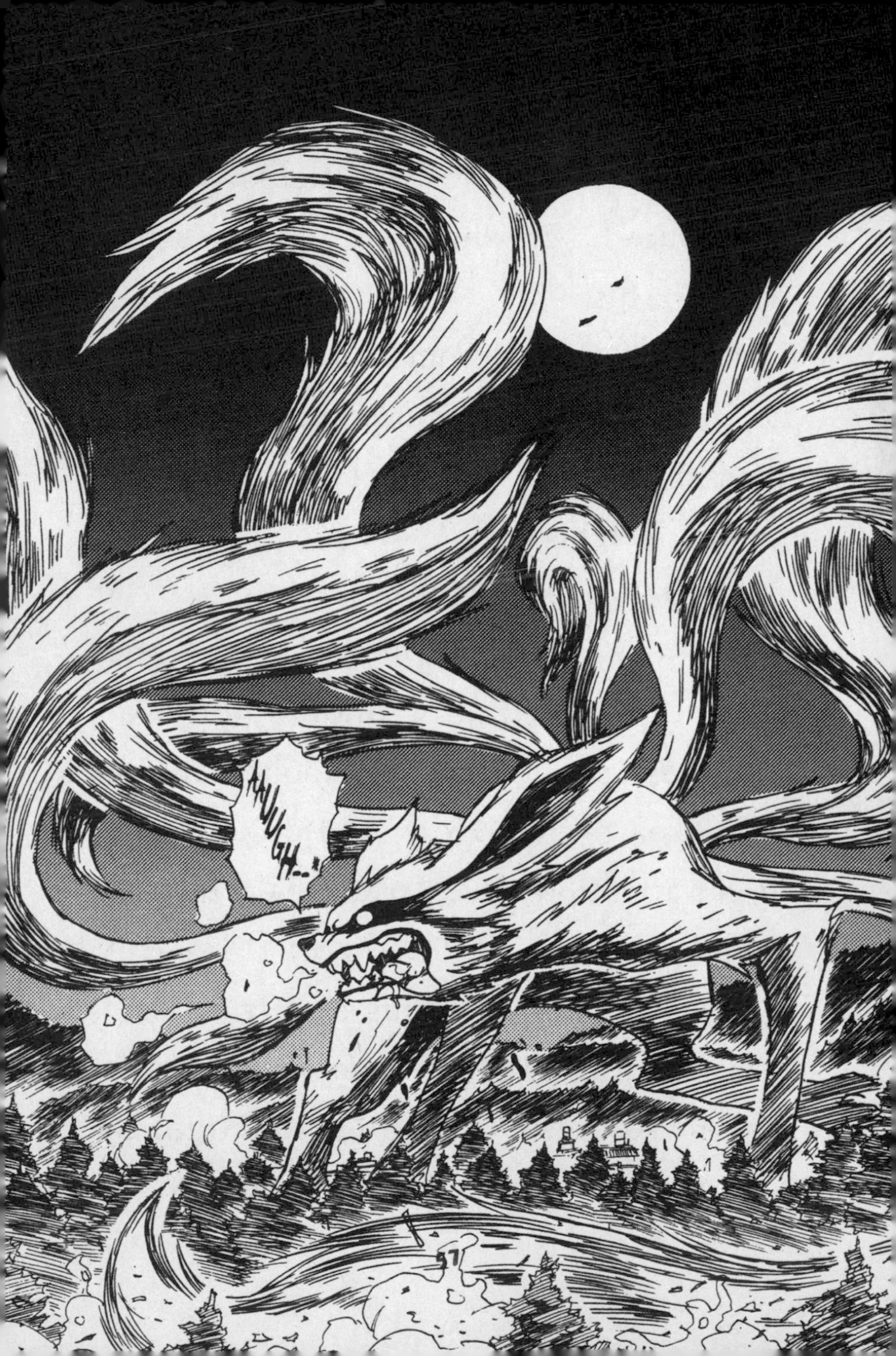
AAUUGH..!!

stunned, helpless—just as Mizuki wanted him. Once he got rid of Naruto, the scroll would be his.

A single tear fell from Naruto's eye. With it, twelve years of loneliness, pain, and rage poured out of his body. He pounded the ground with his feet.

"NOOOOOOO!"

Iruka watched helplessly as the boy cried out. He finally understood Naruto. For years no one had looked at him or spoken to him. He would do anything to get attention—even if it meant pulling stupid pranks.

From the corner of his eye, Iruka saw Mizuki hurl the big throwing star at Naruto. A surge of strength flowed through

Master Iruka. He yanked the last few kunai from the wood, freeing himself.

"Naruto, watch out!" Iruka yelled.

NARUTO HEARD MASTER Iruka call his name. He looked up to see his teacher diving at him. Iruka covered Naruto's body with his own just as the shuriken struck. The weapon hit Iruka instead of Naruto.

Naruto was shocked. His teacher had saved him. **"Why?"** Naruto asked.

"When my parents died, nobody cared about me," Iruka replied. His voice was faint. "I became the class clown, just to get attention. Being the class clown was better than being a nobody."

Tears streamed from Iruka's eyes as he remembered. "You must have been so lonely…"

"Forgive me, Naruto," Iruka said. "I should have been a better sensei. I shouldn't have been so hard on you."

Naruto didn't know what to think. He

didn't know which teacher to trust.

So he ran. He raced through the trees as fast as he could.

Mizuki watched him go and just laughed.

"Did you see that look in his eyes, Iruka?" Mizuki asked. "He's got the eyes of the Demon Fox. He'll use that scroll to take revenge on the village."

Iruka slowly sat up. "You don't know Naruto at all."

Mizuki jumped down from the tree. "I don't have to know him. He got the scroll for me, and that's all I need," he said. "I'll finish you later."

Then he ran off to catch Naruto.

Lord Hokage looked into a crystal ball. His ninja searched for Naruto, but no one found him. Now word had spread through the village. More men were out looking for the boy. The situation was very serious indeed.

Finally, the ball showed Lord Hokage what he was looking for. He saw the scene in the woods. He heard Mizuki's cruel words to Naruto. He saw Iruka save Naruto's life and watched the boy run away.

"Mizuki has pushed Naruto too far," the Hokage said. "There is terrible power locked inside that boy. If that power escapes, our village will be in danger again. And now the secret scroll is in his hands…"

Lord Hokage closed his eyes. Iruka was hurt. There was no one to help Naruto now.

Unless the boy could save himself.

Naruto raced through the woods, still

carrying the scroll on his back. Iruka ran after him, catching up quickly.

"Give me the scroll!" Iruka shouted. "Mizuki is coming after you. He wants it for himself!"

Naruto jumped up onto a tree branch to avoid Iruka. His teacher jumped up next to him. They continued to race from branch to branch.

Suddenly, Naruto jumped off his branch. He delivered a solid kick to Iruka's chest. His teacher cried out as he tumbled from the high branch, slamming into the ground below.

Naruto fell too. He leaned against a tree trunk, panting.

Iruka struggled to get to his knees. His dark eyes blazed with anger.

"How did you know, Naruto?" he asked. "How did you know—I'm not Iruka!"

Iruka changed back into Mizuki.

Naruto just smiled. "I know because *I* am Iruka!"

Naruto changed—into Iruka! Naruto's teacher had changed into Naruto to fool Mizuki.

The *real* Naruto watched them from a hiding place behind a nearby tree. He clutched the scroll tightly to his chest.

Mizuki slowly walked toward Iruka. Iruka was still in a lot of pain from his wounds. The race through the woods had drained all of Iruka's energy. He was helpless against Mizuki now.

"How noble of you to save the life of your

parents' attacker," he said. "You think you and Naruto are alike. But you are wrong. Naruto and I are two of a kind."

"You and Naruto?" Iruka asked.

"I will use the scroll to achieve ultimate power," Mizuki said. "And Naruto will use the power of the scroll to destroy the village. I know you think so too, deep down in your heart."

Naruto felt a sting of pain in his heart. So Iruka really did hate him.

"You are right," Iruka said slowly. "I didn't accept Naruto before. But I do now. **HE'S AN EXCELLENT STUDENT.** He works hard even when others *don't* accept him. And he knows what it's like to be lonely. That boy is no longer the Demon Fox. **HE IS NARUTO UZUMAKI OF**

THE LEAF VILLAGE!"

Tears streamed down Naruto's face as he listened to his teacher. He wasn't confused anymore. He knew who he was—and what he had to do.

Mizuki had a sneer on his face. "Well, isn't that sweet," he said. "You know, Iruka, I was going to save you for last. But sometimes, things don't work out the way you plan. So say good-bye!"

Mizuki took another windmill shuriken from his back. He spun it in his hand, building up speed.

So this is it, Iruka thought. He fixed his eyes on the shuriken, unafraid.

Naruto sprang from his hiding place and kicked Mizuki in the chin as hard as he could.

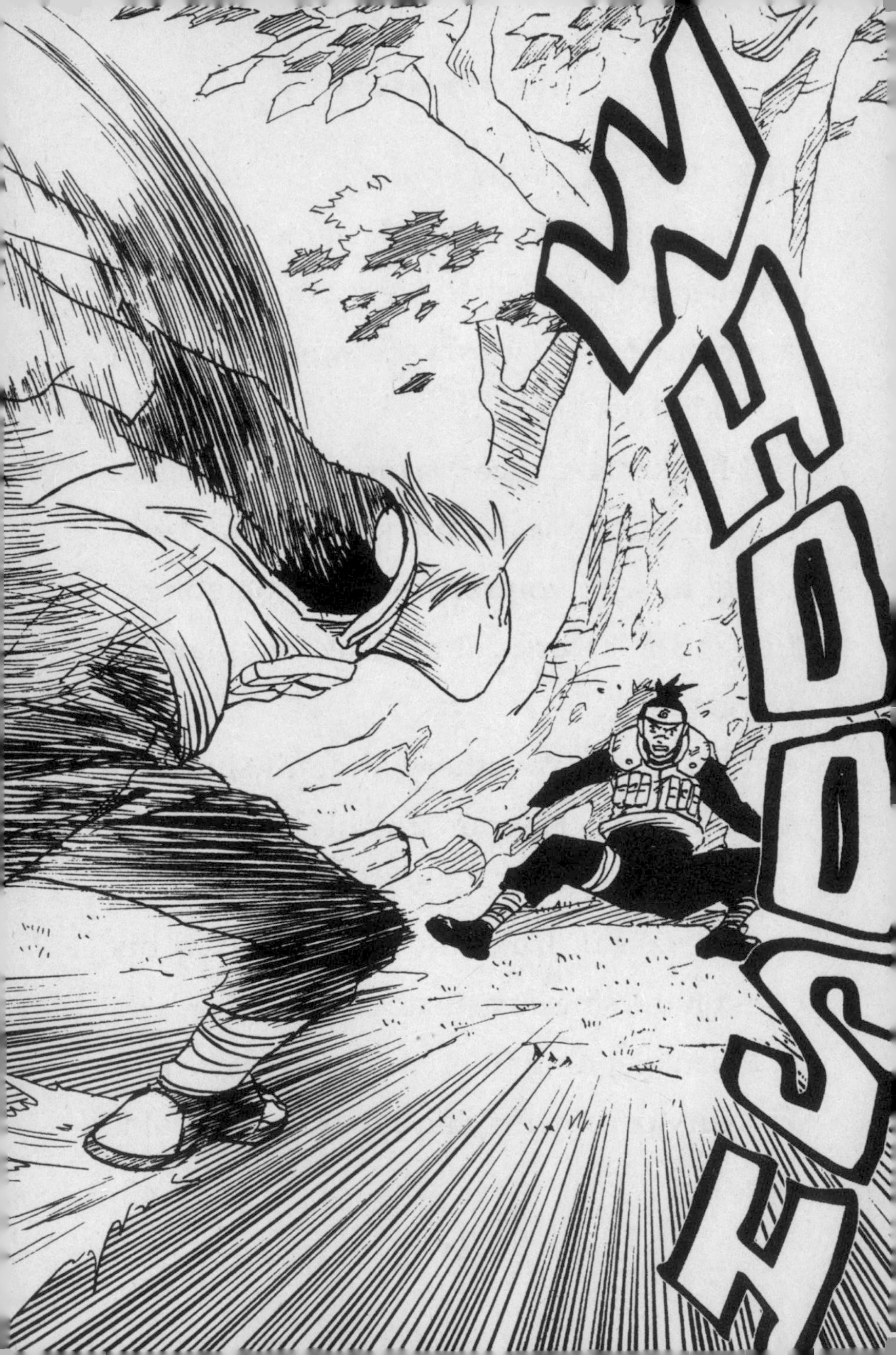
WHOOSH

The windmill shuriken flew from Mizuki's hands. It zoomed away to the side, slicing off a tree branch.

Naruto stood in front of a stunned Mizuki, glaring.

"Keep away from Master Iruka," he said. "Or I will take you down."

"Naruto, get out of here! Save yourself!" Iruka pleaded.

Mizuki was furious now. "Loudmouth brat! I can destroy you with one blow."

"Bring it on, you jerk!" Naruto said. "Anything you try, you'll get it back a thousand times worse."

"You're welcome to try, little fox!" Mizuki shouted.

Mizuki reached for another shuriken.

Iruka closed his eyes. He could face his own end, but not Naruto's.

Then, instead of the whirl of the shuriken, Iruka heard a loud **BONG** ring through the forest. He heard Naruto cry out.

"SHADOW DOPPELGANGER JUTSU!"

Iruka opened his eyes, and he couldn't believe what he saw.

"Naruto?" he gasped.

THE FOREST WAS filled with hundreds of Narutos. They covered every inch of ground. They sat on every tree branch. They surrounded Mizuki on all sides.

Iruka couldn't believe it. Naruto, the boy who could not make one doppelganger, had made an entire army of them.

Mizuki stared at the endless Narutos, shocked. All of the Narutos began to shout at once.

"Over here!"

"Come and get me!"

"What's the matter, tough guy?" Naruto called out. "You said you could destroy me with one blow. What are you waiting for?"

Mizuki was confused.

"Oh well," Naruto said. "Guess I'll have to attack you, then!"

The army of Narutos jumped on Mizuki at once. Iruka watched, shaking his head.

Doppelgangers are only illusions. But Naruto has created real-life copies of himself. He has figured out one of the most difficult ninja arts in just one night! Maybe he will *become a great Hokage someday.*

The dust cleared. Mizuki lay on the ground in a heap, groaning. The hundreds of Narutos disappeared, leaving only the real one.

He looked down at Mizuki.

"Oh well," he said. "I guess I got carried away."

"Naruto, come here," Iruka said. "I've got something for you."

Naruto obeyed, but he felt nervous. He hadn't known the scroll was so dangerous when he took it. He used it to learn a secret jutsu. Was he in trouble?

"Close your eyes," Iruka said.

Uh-oh, Naruto thought. He closed his eyes. This couldn't be good.

Naruto felt Iruka tie something around his head. "Can I open my eyes now?"

"Yes, Naruto. Open your eyes."

Naruto opened his eyes to see Iruka's smiling face.

"CONGRATULATIONS, GRADUATE!"

Iruka shouted.

Naruto reached up. He could feel the shape of a leaf engraved on the metal plate. Iruka wasn't kidding. He had earned his leaf headband. Naruto was a ninja now!

"Let's go get some ramen to celebrate," Iruka said.

Naruto didn't know what to say. He threw his arms around Iruka, giving him a big hug.

"Ow, that hurts!" Iruka protested. "Anyway, I was going to give you a speech about being a ninja. Things are only going to get harder. But I guess that speech can wait until we get to the restaurant."

Naruto wasn't worried. Maybe things

would get harder. But that didn't matter.

He was Naruto Uzumaki, a ninja, and nobody could take that away from him!

Ninja Terms

Hokage
The leader and protector of the Village Hidden in the Leaves. Only the strongest and wisest ninja can achieve this rank.

Jutsu
Jutsu means "arts" or "techniques." Sometimes referred to as *ninjutsu*, which means more specifically the jutsu of a ninja.

Bunshin
Translated as "doppelganger," this is the art of creating multiple versions of yourself.

Sensei
Teacher

Shuriken
A ninja weapon,
a throwing star

Author/artist **Masashi Kishimoto** was born in 1974 in rural Okayama Prefecture, Japan. After spending time in art college, he won the Hop Step Award for new manga artists with his manga *Karakuri* (Mechanism). Kishimoto decided to base his next story on traditional Japanese culture. His first version of *Naruto*, drawn in 1997, was a one-shot story about fox spirits; his final version, which debuted in *Weekly Shonen Jump* in 1999, quickly became the most popular ninja manga in Japan. This book is based on that manga.

The Story of Naruto continues in:
Chapter Book 2
The Tests of a Ninja

After graduating from Ninja Academy, Naruto makes new friends, pretty and smart Sakura and the moody Sasuke. He also meets his new sensei, Kakashi. Naruto's jokester ways may not help him to keep up with his talented new pals. If he wants to be the best ninja ever, he's going to have to work for it!

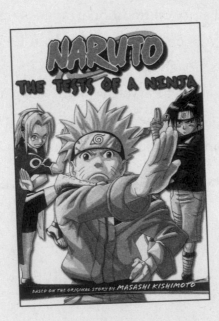